W9-BRT-109

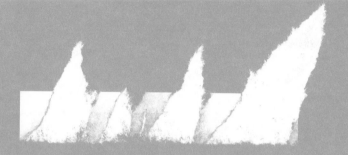

My Body Belongs To Me

Jill Starishevsky

with illustrations by Sara Muller

 **Safety Star Media**

Published by Safety Star Media.

Edited by: Christiane Kafka

For information regarding permission, write to:
Safety Star Media
Attn: Permissions Department
P.O. Box 427, New York, NY 10156

www.SafetyStarMedia.com
www.MyBodyBelongsToMe.com

Library of Congress Control Number: 2008909323

ISBN: 978-0-9821216-0-3

Printed in the United States of America

For Ted, Ally and Becca, the loves of my life.
And for T.T., whose courage beyond her years
became my inspiration.

-J.S.

For Ruby, Sydney and Adie.

–S.M.

Acknowledgements

Special thanks to Robert T. Johnson, Bronx County District Attorney, who has given me the opportunity to do the job I love, and to Elisa Koenderman and Joseph Muroff, former and current chiefs of the Bronx County District Attorney's Child Abuse and Sex Crimes Bureau, respectively, whose guidance and support have been instrumental in my development as a prosecutor.

Thanks also to Pamela Pine from Stop the Silence, for her wealth of information about child sexual abuse; to Jeff Schlanger from SmartVolunteer, whose genius with the Internet has been a valued contribution to this and other projects; and to Melissa Yamello from Storybook Studio, for designing the Safety Star Media logo. Thanks to Sara Muller for bringing this story to life with her beautiful illustrations, and to my family for their feedback and constant support. And of course, thanks to my husband and biggest fan, Ted, who is my collaborator and partner in all ways, and is forever helping me to multitask.

A portion of all proceeds from the sale of this book will be donated to organizations dedicated to the prevention of child sexual abuse.

About the Book

As a prosecutor of child abuse and sex crimes in New York City for more than a decade, I have often encountered children who were sexually abused for lengthy periods of time and suffered in silence. One case in particular had a profound impact on me and compelled me to write this book.

I prosecuted the case of a 9-year-old girl who had been raped by her stepfather since she was 6. She told no one.

One day, the girl saw an episode of "The Oprah Winfrey Show" about children who were physically abused. The episode, "Tortured Children," empowered the girl with this simple message: *If you are being abused, tell your parents. If you can't tell your parents, go to school and tell your teacher.* The girl got the message and *the very next day* went to school and told her teacher. I prosecuted the case for the District Attorney's office. The defendant was convicted and is now serving a lengthy prison sentence.

I have thought often of that very sweet, very brave 9-year-old girl. It occurred to me that after three painful years, all it took to end her nightmare was a TV program encouraging her to "tell a teacher."

I wrote *My Body Belongs to Me* to continue that message. It endeavors to teach children that they don't have to endure abuse in silence. Parents and educators should use it as a tool to facilitate an open dialogue with youngsters. It is my hope that by educating girls and boys about this taboo subject, *My Body Belongs to Me* will prevent them from becoming victims in the first place.

Jill Starishevsky

This is my body,
and it belongs just to me.

I have knees and elbows
and lots of parts you see.

Other parts I have
are not in open view.

I call them my private parts,
of course you have them too.

Mom and Dad once told me
I was their little gem,

and if someone hurt me
to always come to them.

One day when we were visiting

my Uncle Johnny's house,

I was playing with some toys,

quiet as a mouse.

My uncle's friend came over

and sat down next to me,

and touched me in that place

that no one else can see.

I got so scared I froze
and just stayed where I sat.

I thought: This is MY body!
Why did he do that?

He said it's our secret
and told me not to tell.

But I ran away real fast
and then began to yell.

I told my Mom and Dad
what just had taken place.

They said that I was really brave
and then each kissed my face.

Mom and Dad said they were proud
I told them right away.

It made me feel better, too —
they believed what I had to say.

I learned if I was too scared
to tell my Mom or Dad,

I could have told my teacher
what made me feel so sad.

I know it wasn't my fault
and I did nothing wrong.

This is my body,
and I'm growing big and strong.

Dear Reader,

Among the first things we teach children is to name the various parts of their bodies. As they grow older, this conversation should go a step further – some parts of their bodies are private and belong just to them.

Just as we teach youngsters what to do in case of fire, we must teach them what to do if someone touches them inappropriately. The overriding message of *My Body Belongs to Me* is that if someone touches you, tell.

Sadly, the overwhelming majority of sexually abused children don't immediately disclose the abuse. As a result, the abuse often escalates. There are many reasons for a child's silence: Perhaps the abuser says it's a secret. Maybe the child believes that he or she is at fault. Without being taught that his or her body has boundaries, a child may be too young to understand that the abuse is wrong.

Parents often don't know when or how to approach this topic with their children. Written for 3-to-10-year-olds, *My Body Belongs to Me* is a tool that aims to facilitate this difficult discussion in a straightforward yet sensitive manner.

Jill Starishevsky

Suggestions for the Storyteller

The following are some tips to make this subject approachable for children.

1. Use the story as a tool to begin a conversation with your child. Address the topic periodically to reinforce the message.

2. Teach children the correct terms for their body parts. Enable them to use language that will make them comfortable talking to you.

3. Ask the child: What would you do if someone touched you on your _____? Who would you tell? Why is it important to tell? What would you do if the person said it was "our secret"? Encourage the child to say they would tell a parent or a teacher right away because it's their body.

4. Discuss the importance of the rule "no secrets." Put this rule into practice: If someone, even a grandparent, says something to your child like, "I'll get you an ice cream later, but it will be our secret," firmly but politely say, "We don't do secrets in our family." Then turn to your child and repeat, "We don't do secrets. We can tell each other everything."

5. Keep in mind, especially when reading the book in a group setting, that you may be reading to a child who has already been touched in some way and is keeping it a secret. Be sensitive and avoid making the child feel guilty for not having told right away. Convey that it is OK for the child to tell someone even if he or she has been keeping it a secret for a long time.

6. Encourage your children to tell you about things that happen to them that make them feel scared, sad or uncomfortable. If children have an open line of communication, they will be more inclined to alert you to something inappropriate early on.

7. Encourage your children to trust their feelings – if something doesn't feel right, they should get away as soon as possible and tell you about it.

Where To Find Help

Darkness to Light®
1-866-FOR-LIGHT   www.darkness2light.org

Darkness to Light's mission is to shift responsibility for preventing child sexual abuse from children to adults by providing information on how to prevent, recognize and react responsibly to child sexual abuse.

Love Our Children USA™
1-888-347-KIDS   www.loveourchildrenusa.org

Love Our Children USA is the national nonprofit leader in breaking the cycle of violence against children. Since 1999, Love Our Children USA has paved the way in the prevention of all forms of violence and neglect against children, keeping children safe and strengthening families.

National Center for Missing & Exploited Children (NCMEC)
1-800-THE-LOST   www.missingkids.com

NCMEC is a public-private partnership serving as a national clearinghouse for information on missing children and the prevention of child victimization. NCMEC works in conjunction with the U.S. Department of Justice's Office of Juvenile Justice and Delinquency Prevention.

RAINN

1-800-656-HOPE   www.rainn.org

RAINN (Rape, Abuse & Incest National Network) is the nation's largest anti-sexual assault organization. RAINN created the National Sexual Assault Hotlines, which it operates in partnership with more than 1,100 local rape crisis centers across the country. RAINN also carries out programs to prevent sexual assault, help victims and ensure that rapists are brought to justice.

Stop It Now!®

1-888-PREVENT   www.stopitnow.org

Stop It Now! offers adults the tools they need to prevent sexual abuse before a child is harmed. They provide support, information and resources that enable individuals and families to keep children safe and create healthier communities. In collaboration with a network of community-based programs, they reach out to adults who are concerned about their own or others' sexualized behavior toward children.

Stop the Silence: Stop Child Sexual Abuse, Inc.®

301-464-4791   www.stopcsa.org

Stop the Silence works with others toward the prevention and treatment of child sexual abuse. The worldwide mission of Stop the Silence is to expose and stop child sexual abuse, help survivors heal, and celebrate the lives of those healed.

About the Author and the Illustrator

Jill Starishevsky is an Assistant District Attorney in New York City, where she has prosecuted hundreds of sex offenders and dedicated her career to seeking justice for victims of child abuse and sex crimes. Outside the courtroom, Jill's fondness for writing led her to create thepoemlady.com, where she pens personalized pieces. Her mission to protect children, along with her penchant for poetry, inspired *My Body Belongs to Me*. A mother of two, Jill is also founder of HowsMyNanny.com, a service that enables parents to purchase a license plate for their child's stroller so the public can report positive or negative nanny observations.

Sara Muller's lifelong love of art and design inspired her to put paint to paper for the drawings in *My Body Belongs to Me*. Sara, whose creative drive developed into a career in journalism, has made her mark as a reporter, writer and producer. Her work has appeared on the Food Network, MSNBC and ABC News. She lives in New York City with her husband and their two daughters.